Valerie ©1978

Grindle Lamfoon

Grin' del   Lam foon'

and the

Procurnious Fleekers

Pro kur' nee us   Flee' kurs

Grindle Lamfoon
and the
Procurnious Fleekers

Valerie Hubbard Damon

**First published in the United States of America in 1979 by
Star Publications, PO Box 22534, Kansas City, Missouri 64113.**

Library of Congress Catalog Card Number 78-64526

Damon, Valerie Hubbard

Grindle Lamfoon and the Procurnious Fleekers

Kansas City, Missouri: Star Publications

ISBN 0-932356-14-1
ISBN 0-932356-05-2 (lib. bdg.)

Star Publications
PO Box 22534
Kansas City, Missouri 64113
816-523-8228

Second Edition

In memory of Vertigo,
(my parakeet friend)

Grindle Lamfoon and the Procurnious Fleekers
is dedicated to all who made its creation
possible, especially the trees.

There once was an evening
so quiet and pleasing.
It appeared quite still,
 just as still as could be.
T'was not the case,
 for down at the base
 of a mellow,
 big Mellow Leaf Tree,
 was a curious sight
 concerning the plight
 of a tiny Procurnious Fleeker.
Now Procurnious Fleekers
 are funny bird creatures
 living in towns
 in shapely tall homes.
There are doctors and artists
 and nice teacher fleekers.
The cooks make the best goodies
 that you've ever known.
Now...
 Let's go to the place
 by the Mellow Tree base,
 where our story is now to begin...

It's dark and it's still
and there on a hill
in a shadowy light so dim,
one Procurnious Fleeker,
downcast and befumed,
mourns his poor plight
by the light of the moon.
"Oh, Moon! Moon! MOON!.
so befumed I am doomed!."
cried our Procurnious Fleeker,
called Grindle Lamfoon.
"Tomorrow is May Day
and all other Fleekers
will have costumes with horns
and marvelous bleekers
and I will have nothing !!!
I'm poor and can't buy
a costume with jingles
and baubles and ties
that will look so amusing
with connections and fusings.
Oh !! ... Moon! Moon! Moon!
I am doomed !!"

"Not so!" said the moon
   in a tune.
"What's that? Who are you?!!"
   said Grindle Lamfoon.
"Up here in the sky,
   a most obvious place
   for a face on the moon
   to be talking!"
"Talking?...hmmm..Talking!!"
Grindle sat gawking
   at the round
   smiling face in the sky.
"See what there is,"
   said the moon in a tune
   with a melody sweet
   and quite pleasing.
"See what there is??? Humph!!"
   Grindle flashed back a frown
   to that goon of a moon
   singing tunes!

"Stop teasing, stop teasing!
You're not at all pleasing.
I'm doomed and befumed
 and you sing silly tunes!!"
"Be still," said the moon,
 "and listen to me.
Listen .. be quiet ..
 and soon you will see.
Now ...
 look up above
 and look down below
 beside and behind.
Let your mind growww!"

Our Procurnious Fleeker,
Grindle Lamfoon,
  looked behind, beside
  and up at the moon.
His eyes became larger,
  his face began smiling !!!
He rushed here and there,
  began piling and piling
  flowers and leaves
  and sticks and seeds !
Why, all around him
  lay marvelous beads
  and things that would bauble
  and jingle and bloom,
  such marvelous tweekers
  for Grindle Lamfoon !
"These things from the woods
  are much greater by far
  than expensive made costumes
  and Fleeker-made cars."

Grindle worked all the night
with flowers and blooms
  making bleekers and norns
  with gigantic plumes
  and all made of flowers,
  of leaves and of seeds.
The fusings were vines
  and marvelous weeds,
  free natural things
  from such obvious places.
Grindle had strung tiny seeds
  to make laces,
  and hung large bell flowers
  in the strangest of places.

His tarpers were threaded...
by dawn he was ready.
The bells and bafoonels
   were all holding steady.
Slowly and singing
   came Grindle Lamfoon,
   the Procurnious Fleeker
   inspired by the moon,
   up to the place
   by the Mellow Leaf Tree
   where all the town Fleekers
   came just to see...

the May Day Parade
of baubles and bleekers,
befits and bafoons,
pronurns and betweekers,
Procurnious Pie and Fleeker Popcorn,
red, yellow and pink procusganorns.
Oh, such a dazzling sight to behold!
Then all became quiet...
and up the hill strolled
Grindle Lamfoon,
the smallest of Fleekers,
with the largest and strangest
costume and bleekers.
Oh, it was truly a sight to behold,
to see little Grindle
acting so bold
and pulling his bloom-jingling
baubles and lorns
with pink and red fusings
and yellow-gold horns.
And right on the side
of the giant bafoon
was a hand-painted plaque
of the moon with a tune.

Procurnious Fleekers were
scurrying about,
  singing and laughing
  and giving great shouts
  of praise and amazement
  to Grindle Lamfoon
  who sang *a great song*
  like the moon with his tune.
The biggest blue ribbon
  for the flobbeling lorns,
  the loudest betweekers
  and impressive ganorns
  naturally went to Grindle Lamfoon,
  the same little Fleeker
  inspired by the moon.

And Grindle remembers
to this very day...
the moon singing tunes
and what he had to say
of looking beside,
behind, and around,
by looking all over
there's lots to be found!
"See what there is,"
said the moon in a tune.
"What a wonderful song,"
thought Grindle Lamfoon.